The Light Won't Go Out

A Collection of Short Stories and Poems

To Support Children's Cancer

Printed in the United States of America

First Edtition, 2016

10 9 8 7 6 5 4 3 2 1

About Makin Books Publishing

Makin Books strives to accomplish something that other publishers don't. Teamwork. Working side by side with their authors they offer a variety of stories giving new and old authors a platform to stand on. They stay with their authors all the way, helping them to grow.

Makin Books and its authors have come together and donated their time and stories for this collection all for a great cause. This year Makin Books will be donating all profits to the Charity This Star Won't Go Out www.tswgo.org

This Star Won't Go Out supports families with children that have cancer by providing funds to help pay for travel, a mortgage or rent check, and other cost of living expenses. This helps take the burden of the families.

This holiday season Makin Books will also be supporting This Star Won't Go Out to help families during the holiday season.

Douglas Debelak

Douglas Debelak has a degree in philosophy. He put his literary aspirations on hold when he became a father and taught himself how to write software instead to support his family. He has had a successful career as a software engineer, but always promised himself he'd return to his dream of writing a novel. His debut novel, The Involuntary Ghostwriter, the first book in a trilogy is scheduled to be published by Makin Books Publishing later this year. The second, Long Life and Prosperity, will follow soon after, and the conclusion, Forever is a Very Long Time, is well under way.

He does live with his wife in a beautiful old house, in a wonderful historic neighborhood. There is an annual Christmas tour. They have had beautiful 'real' trees every Christmas since the first time their house was on the tour.

A Tale of Two Trees

Christmas trees these days are so realistic that we now have to make a point of saying, that's a real tree. Some people will still say, "But, it doesn't smell real," even as 'real' trees become ever more rare and the person questioning the reality of our tree may only have a scent from a spray can or candle to compare, or, if they are old enough, a memory from years long past.

For years, recently, when our tree was not 'real', but realistic enough that many people assumed it had to be 'real', we'd silenced the criticisms that it didn't smell 'real' by stuffing real pine boughs in between the artificial, and guests would touch the 'artificial' needles, insist they were real, and ask where we managed to find such perfect trees, year in and year out. I suspect that some of our guests conjured nostalgic memories of years past, when families made a day of going out into the woods together to search for and bring home the perfect tree, still fresh with running sap. Then, when we broke the news that the tree was, in fact, 'artificial', they'd want to know how we'd found such a perfect 'artificial' tree.

So, why go to the trouble of having a 'real' tree?

Every year, the 'artificial' tree had to be dug out from under everything that had been stacked on top of it over the past twelve months and dragged up from the basement. The tree originally came in two boxes, each of which weighed close to 100 lbs., one slightly more and the other slightly less. The boxes had to be dragged, hefted, or walked on end, to the bottom of the basement stairs, then lifted up one stair at a time to the first floor, and then dragged, hefted, or walked end on end, again into the living room. After which, the pieces had to be assembled, which again required lifting, first from the boxes, then the top pieces had to be placed atop the lower. There were either two or three piece pieces, depending whether we wanted an eight or eleven-foot tree. My vote was always eight, my wife's eleven, and I was out voted.

I'd be soaked in sweat and exhausted every year by the time I'd assembled the tree. And, every year, the Monday following required a trip to the Chiropractor. Another trip to the Chiropractor was scheduled for the first or second Monday in the new year after taking down the tree and hauling the boxes back to the basement. At least hauling the boxes back to the basement was downhill.

Doesn't a 'real' tree require every bit as much work, you may ask, maybe more? No, there are companies who, for a hefty price, will deliver a perfect 'real' tree every year, name the size and type of tree, then they'll come and haul it away afterward. Yes, I have to string lights for the 'real' tree, which hadn't been necessary with the pre-lite 'artificial' tree, and this is a pain in the behind, but it also doesn't require two annual trips to the Chiropractor.

What about the mess, with all the needles, especially when the tree is delivered, then again when it is hauled away? The trees come in a bag, which is pulled down and spread out to become a tree skirt after trees are delivered and placed in the tree stand. Then the tree skirt becomes a bag again when the tree is hauled away, keeping all the needles, or at least most of them, inside.

Watering the tree, which had initially required getting down on the floor, twice a day, and shimmying under the tree on my back with a watering can, was just as likely to require a trip to the Chiropractor during the holidays. But, I solved this by buying a funnel, meant for changing oil, from the automotive department of the local hardware store. The bottom end goes into the tree stand and the funnel end is hidden – found one that is green – in the tree far enough not to be easily seen, but near enough to easily reach it with the watering can. Ta-Da!

Here is another little trick. To determine whether I have the lights strung so that the tree is uniformly lit, I take off my glasses. Everything becomes a blur, except the dark spots, which need more lights.

So, now that I have sucked all the romance and Christmas spirit out of the Christmas tree experience, I feel I should try to return some of it to you.

~~~

A number of years back, my wife and I became fortunate enough to own a beautiful old historic Victorian home, in a historic neighborhood, which has a well-known annual Christmas house tour. The tour has been listed in at least one edition of the book, 'A Thousand Things to Do Before You Die'. Several times now, my wife and I have agreed to be on the tour and open our home to nearly two-thousand people, who pay money, to 'ooh' and 'awe' over the decorations, the original crown molding, the finely crafted woodwork, the antique lighting fixtures and chandeliers (originally gas, now electric), the mantles, the mirrors, furniture and artwork.

The money from the tour had been used to purchase derelict properties that remained in the neighborhood, renovate them structurally, fix the roof, re-point the brick, and update the plumbing, electric, etc., so they were ready to sell to someone willing to take on the renovation from there, which was much less daunting than taking it on from the start. Very few of these derelict properties remain, so the money is now used to improve the neighborhood in other ways.

Back to Christmas trees, even though it has proven to be less work, the real reason we decided to have a 'real' tree again, and discovered that it was less work, was that we felt we owed the people coming through our home the honest article. After all, we've gone to great effort to make sure the mirror above the mantle, the lighting fixtures, and key pieces of furniture were not only period appropriate in appearance, but the genuine article.

During the house tour, the home owners, or their representatives, are present to tell the story of their homes and answer questions. Nearly all of the home owners in the neighborhood have had house histories compiled by a local 'house historian' and know when their house was built, who built it, what they paid for the lot it was built on, and every person who has owned it since.

Included in the house histories are the stories of some of the people who've lived in the house in years past, summarized from newspaper articles of the day. It is a common sentiment amongst the home owners in the neighborhood that we are just the current custodians of these houses. They were here long before us and will have other custodians long after we are gone. I find that both humbling and another troubling reminder of my mortality.

The tour takes place early in December, on a Friday evening, from 6pm to 9pm, and again on Saturday, from noon until 9pm, with new groups of

30 or more people arriving approximately every 15 minutes. Even though it is a long time to be on my feet these days, and my voice is gone by Saturday evening at 9pm, I feel it is my responsibility to be present and tell the story of our home to every group.

I tell them that our home is one of the oldest in the neighborhood. The house was built by a husband and wife, Robert and Martha **Graham** at the beginning of the American Civil War, when Abraham Lincoln was President. It was built on property that had been subdivided into lots in 1858. Once upon a time, for at least a short time, our house sat alone in the middle of what had once been a cow pasture. The deed for the lot was registered to Martha, who purchased it in 1861 for $450.

Robert and Martha had a daughter, also Martha, who was known as Mattie. Mattie Graham became of one of the leading educators of her time. She was the first woman to be a high school principal in the United States. Andrew Mellon was one of her students. Andrew Carnegie was a personal friend, who spoke at her funeral. Over the course of a few decades following our house being built, the neighborhood became the wealthiest in the world. So, there were many, now famous, wealthy people living within a few blocks radius, the wealth coming from steel and supporting industries, such as coal and railroads.

Beginning in the early 1900s, the wealthy began to abandon the neighborhood, to areas further away from soot and bad air from the steel mills that had created their wealth. The abandonment accelerated as the automobile became more common. Over the course of the first half of the 20th century, the neighborhood declined, eventually becoming just another part of the urban intercity. Many of the homes were turned into apartments, or boarding houses, where walls were built in the middle of windows to subdivide rooms, and no concern was given to preserving architectural details.

A number of mansions still exist in the neighborhood, but unfortunately many of the grandest homes were destroyed, during those years when there was no concern for historical preservation. Some were destroyed to make way for a community college, others to make way for highways and ramps to help facilitate the escape from the city. Some burned down, leaving only vacant lots. Some were abandoned, leaving shells, without roofs, windows, doors or any of the architectural features that it was possible to remove. Mantles and fireplace surrounds were gone. Fine woodwork, doors and stair railings were gone. Dirt and dust from decaying brick and plaster were left.

Then, beginning in the early 1970s, brave, crazy people, many of them still our current neighbors, began returning and buying the shells and ruins to restore and live in them. False walls were torn down. Original walls were stripped down to the studs and brick. People learned how to plaster, the old fashion way, not just nailing up drywall. They learned to repoint brick, to repair chimneys and external walls, along with roofing, plumbing, woodworking and electrical work. And, of course, there was endless painting. In some instances, rather than try to learn it all, they traded labor. I'll help you point your brick, if you help me replace my sewer and water pipes, or upgrade my electrical service.

Since it wasn't the best of neighborhoods at the time and none of the homes were in the best of shape, many were purchased for only a few thousand dollars or less. And, while most of the new owners had the opportunity to completely modernize their homes, instead nearly every one of them decided to restore their homes as close as possible to the original - with modern comforts of course. No one, so far as I know, opted for outhouses for the sake of authenticity.

Restoration of the houses to their original state was difficult or impossible in most instances, since so much of what had originally been there was gone. But, not all of it was gone. A fair amount was just somewhere else. Some pieces were found in other homes, in other parts of the city, some of which, although newer, were now derelict as well. Some were found leaning against walls in abandoned warehouses. Some in the possession of antiques dealers.

These new neighbors went on a cooperative quest. "Hey, I think I found you a mantle that will fit in your living room." In a surprising number of instances, the original mantles from the homes were found. This could be determined, because they'd also gone on a cooperative quest to find and share old pictures from the neighborhood. In one instance, one of the neighbors found one of a matching set of grand mantles that had originally come from his home, then several years later he spotted the twin in the back of a pickup truck driving through the neighborhood. He gave chase and was able to recover the second of the matching mantles as well.

Many of these homes are now valued at a hundred or more times their purchase price in the 1970s. Multiples created by sweat equity. Of course, now 'gentrification' has become a bad word in some circles.

My wife tells me I ramble and talk too much when talking about our home and our wonderful neighborhood – and it isn't only the beautifully restored homes that make it wonderful. It is far more the people, of whom I could ramble on about as well.

For example, we met new friends in the neighborhood who had lived in the same city in Germany, when I was working on a project overseas. We had to have bumped into them there, at wine festivals, or just shopping in the market. But, we met at a party in our neighborhood. Small world. We also socialized more in the first year that we lived in the neighborhood than we had in the thirty years previous.

My wife would say I'm rambling, so back to the house tour.

I talk about a number of the pieces in our home, whether lights, mirrors or furniture, and how and where we found them. Often from Craigslist – but I also get yelled at for sharing too much about the 'deals' we've found, rather than let people make the assumption that the mirror above our living room mantle – an antique diamond dust mirror from the 1880s – had to have cost ten-thousand dollars or more, since there are mirrors of the same vintage, and not in as good a condition, in antique shops with such price tags. No, I went with my wife to check out an antique china cabinet that was another of her Craigslist finds. She'll tell you about that when she talks about the dining room. But, I was standing near the front door, anxiously hoping she would hurry, so I could escape – buy the piece or don't already. No, at least an hour of haggling is required – she's not sure whether she really 'loves' the piece, not sure it will fit where she's thinking of putting it. Would you consider a lower offer? While this is going on, I'm daydreaming to escape the agony of my boredom, and realize I'm seeing little sparkles in the corners of this beautiful antique mirror hanging on the wall in the hallway.

I asked, "It that a diamond dust mirror?"

I get a look, because I'm interrupting the haggling.

"Yes, I'm sure it must be, given its age," I'm told.

"Is that for sale as well?"

Now I'm getting death stares. My wife is on a mission. She's locked onto a target. And, now her haggle is losing momentum.

"Everything is for sale. So, yes, the mirror included."

"How much?" I'm already in trouble. So, there is no sense trying to save myself at that point.

"$1000."

"Will you take $500?"

"$600 is as low as I'll go."

"Done."

That's how you haggle, I want to explain. It doesn't require an hour or more of hemming and hawing.

But, then comes the interesting part. How am I going to get this mirror home? The seller is prepared to deliver the china cabinet my wife finally decides to buy, for the price I'm convinced I could have negotiated in 30 seconds, just as I had the mirror. After all, the woman has sold the house. The closing is a few days away. Anything she doesn't sell stays in the house. But, she can't deliver the mirror, because she's not sure how it is mounted on the wall. She has no idea what it weighs.

I'd assisted a friend moving a similar mirror not long before, just from one room to the next, and it had been all we could do to lift it off the floor and shuffle ahead a few feet at a time before we needed to set it down again. It had to have weighed somewhere between three and four-hundred pounds. So, I assumed that would be the case with this mirror I'd just bought as well. I think to myself, I'm going to need to rent a truck and I'm going to need a lot of help. But, where are your buddies when you need them? Busy. Bad back, sorry. One single friend volunteers.

But, I'd paid for the mirror and needed to get it out of the house. So, I found myself, and the single friend who'd volunteered - and actually shown up - bracing ourselves to hold up this mirror, while I reached around behind it with a pair of bolt cutters to cut through the steel cable holding the mirror on the wall. We tried lifting the mirror off the large bolt the cable was looped over - which we'd already been warned wouldn't work, and was why I'd had the foresight to borrow the bolt cutters. As predicted, the mirror didn't budge. I had visions of the mirror crashing down and shattering in the middle of the hallway, but using gravity and trying to soften its landing when it came down was my only hope.

I tried to help brace the mirror with one hip as best I could, in order to have my hands free to use the bolt cutters, because I couldn't expect my friend to handle all that weight himself. I was afraid we wouldn't be able to handle the weight together, even if I did manage to drop the bolt cutters and grab the bottom of the mirror in time.

After a few minute's struggle, I managed to cut the cable, drop the bolt cutters as quickly as I could and caught the bottom of the mirror, just as I'd visualized in my best case scenario. Nothing. The mirror didn't move at all. Crap! I said worse, but I've promised to keep this story PG-13.

Something else had to be holding up the mirror. So, I eased around to see what it could be, and, as I did, the mirror shifted and slid a few inches down the wall. But, my friend, with the help of me still holding on with one hand, was able to hold the mirror from sliding any further, and together we were able to slowly ease it to the floor with nowhere near the effort we'd expected. What I'd expected was far worse than just another Chiropractor visit.

Once the mirror was down, my friend and I lifted it - to make sure we were dealing with reality - shrugged at one another and carried it out to the truck. We figured it couldn't have weighed much more than a hundred pounds. So far, so good.

Once we got the mirror to my house, I faced the next hurdle. When I'd bought it, my wife had immediately asked where I thought I would put this mirror. It was too big to go anywhere in our house. I immediately said, I was going to put it up above the living room mantle.

It would never fit, I was told. I was sure it would.

Had I measured either the mirror or the distance from the mantle to the ceiling?

No. Of course not.

So, my wife was standing with her arms crossed across her chest, smirking, while I set our tall step ladder in place and my friend and I lifted the base of the mirror up onto the mantle. Then I had to climb the ladder, lifting the top end of the mirror as I did, to stand it up and lean it against the wall. It wasn't t going to fit, my wife informed me again, as I climbed the ladder, carefully, since I had to use at least one hand to hold the mirror and had to let go of the ladder entirely at least once every step. She'd told me it wouldn't fit, my wife reiterated each step as well.

It fit. With a quarter inch to spare. According to my wife, I was one lucky #$#$@$%! Again, I promised to keep this PG-13.

Now our mirror and its story are one of the highlights of any tour we give of our house, whether for the Christmas tour, the neighborhood wine tours in the summer, or just new friends wanting to see it for the first time. The mirror immediately transformed and defined our living room. It was meant to be there. Even my wife agrees, no longer begrudgingly, after six or seven years.

There is plenty more to tell about the house, including the story about how I bought it, but I usually have tour guides tapping their watches by the time I finish telling the story of the mirror. They have a schedule to keep. So, I wrap up my presentation, and everyone comments on our beautiful Christmas tree, on their way to the dining room and my wife's presentation. Yes, of course, it's real. And, I hear my wife begin her presentation answering all the questions about the china cabinet I'd told them about. If I was writing this on my phone, I'd add an emoji.

I often flash back, during the Christmas holiday to my childhood, when my life was markedly different, and I could never have imagined standing in front of groups of people, talking about Christmas trees and mirrors.

I remember my first Christmas when we weren't going to have a real tree. At that time, my family, actually just my mother, my siblings and me, could not afford a Christmas tree and were not going to have one at all that year. It would be a clear give away of your age if you are able to remember such things, but there were artificial trees back then, and someone had given us a second hand artificial Christmas tree, that was mostly silver tinsel glued to silver aluminum rods sticking out from an aluminum post.

Now days, anyone who's ever watched Seinfeld, would recognize it as more a Festivus pole than a Christmas tree. There was a device, that came with it, with a light bulb and a rotating multi-color plastic disk to reflect different colors from the tinsel, apparently to make that stark, ugly, fraud of a Christmas tree more festive.

I thought it failed utterly and I believe I was even more depressed that this would be our Christmas than if we'd had no tree at all. My mother felt bad too and apologized, but that was the best we could do that year. We couldn't afford to buy a real tree. Besides, it was Christmas eve and all the real trees would be sold.

I don't remember exactly how old I was, but old enough to have a paper route and three dollars. I was going to get us a 'real' tree. Real trees were… I forget, but considerably more than three dollars. It was already dark. It was bitterly cold. The nearest place selling Christmas trees was at least a mile away. We didn't have a car. There was no way I'd be able walk all that way and drag a tree home myself, even if I did manage to find a Christmas tree someone would sell me for three dollars. I said, I'd take my little brother, who was three years younger. I was determined. So, my mother bundled us up and sent us off into the night with my three dollars in quest of a 'real' Christmas tree.

My mother told me, if I found one, the tree would need to fit in our Christmas tree stand and she gave me the part of the base the tree would need to fit into. It was a metal cylinder with a rounded bottom, that just fit over my gloved fist, like a gauntlet. My brother and I were both afraid to be out in our neighborhood after dark, even if it was too cold for anyone else to be out. So, I was ready to defend us with our Christmas tree holder, if necessary.

We walked, what felt more like ten miles than one. Our feet, hands and faces were numb, and we were both shaking from the cold. The tree place was closing, but the guy selling trees was still there, throwing his remaining trees in the back of his pickup truck. The sign said, 'Close Out. $5'. I told him, I had $3. No, he shook his head, they were $5 and turned back to tossing trees into his truck.

We stood there, too cold and disappointed to move, watching him, and he must have finally felt a little Christmas spirit, looking at two frozen little kids, both on the verge of tears. He pointed to a scrawny, pathetic looking excuse for a Christmas tree that I don't believe he intended to bother throwing into his truck, and told me $3, take it or leave it. I took the cylinder from our Christmas tree holder off my fist and made sure the base of the tree fit. It did with plenty to spare. I handed him my $3 and he jumped in his truck and left, leaving us and the scrawny tree behind, with no thought to, 'Where are you kids going?'

But, we had a 'real' Christmas tree, which my brother and I both recognized years later, while watching the cartoon, Charley Brown's Christmas. Our tree was every bit as pathetic. And, we still had what had seemed a ten-mile hike back home, frozen to the bone, with a Christmas tree the two of us could barely carry, scrawny as it was. I don't remember how long it took us, walking half a block or so before we needed to set the tree down again to rest. We jumped and looked around at every noise. Then trudged a little further. We could barely bend our limbs by the time we got home, and were both so hypothermic it was a wonder we remembered the way.

My mother cried and made us hot chocolate. We had a 'real' tree.

Years later, looking at our splendid, perfect tree and the people looking around in wonder at our home, I do feel blessed beyond measure.

Stephen L. Brayton

Stephen L. Brayton owns and operates Brayton's Black Belt Academy in Oskaloosa, Iowa. He is a Fifth-Degree Black Belt and certified instructor in The American Taekwondo Association. Currently, he is an Assistant Graphic Designer for Gannett Image and Design Company.

He began writing as a child; his first short story concerned a true incident about his reactions to discipline. During high school, he wrote for the school newspaper and was a photographer for the yearbook. For a Mass Media class, he wrote and edited a video project.

In college, he began a personal journal for a writing class; said journal is ongoing. He was also a reporter for the college newspaper. During his early twenties, while working for a Kewanee, Illinois radio station, he wrote a fantasy based story and a trilogy for a comic book.

His current publications include Alpha, a Mallory Petersen mystery, and White Belt Weapons, a Mallory Petersen short story that is included in the Iowa's Original Writers Anthology.

Learn more about Stephen at:

Stephenbrayton.com

stephenbrayton.wordpress.com

braytonsbookbuzz.wordpress.com

Twitter: @SLBrayton

www.facebook.com/stephen.brayton

The Christmas Visit

"Merry Christmas, Darren."

"Merry Christmas, Miss Petersen."

We hugged and I started for the door.

"Don't stay too long. Go home. Be with your family."

He smiled and I left the office. Tomorrow would be December 24th, there would be no clients wanting to hire Mallory Petersen Investigations, but I knew my office manager, Darren, would stay to finish up whatever paperwork he felt needed completion, to clean up, and to double and triple check security.

That's Darren's personality. Loyal, dependable, and courteous. If needed, he'd be at the office Christmas Day. He be there for me.

When I walked outside I saw three more inches of snow in the parking lot. The white stuff had come earlier than expected this year. Yesterday, the temperature had risen to where the streets were slushy. Today, clouds had moved in, the mercury had dropped and snow had fallen at a steady rate for hours.

Unfortunately, the end of the year drop off of cases had hit my private investigations firm a week ago. We had accepted five background checks from companies for new hires in the last ten days, but no cases requiring me to hit the streets.

Winter doldrums set it. Darren and I played board games-or were they bored games-until we all but fell asleep in our chairs. I also own and operate a taekwondo school in Des Moines, so I wrote class schedules for future classes and emailed them to my assistant instructors. The studio was closed for the holiday season and since Christmas fell on a Friday, the students had most of the week off.

I trudged through the snow to my Dodge Dart. Decades old car but the engine fired up on the first try. I merged with the rest of the end of the day traffic, also heading home or to supper or maybe to Christmas parties. My plans were to eat supper, pack some clothes, and come morning, I'd drive to my parents' house in southeast Iowa.

I don't know what it was about this Christmas, but I was tired. I tried to stay positive in class, happy the cases that did come in would pay the bills, but the holiday season had become long and I needed a lift in my spirit. I hoped spending time with my family would do the trick.

Seven minutes after five and the sun was already below the horizon. A string of brake lights told me everybody was being cautious on the slick streets.

Twenty minutes later, I turned onto North Hickory Drive in Pleasant Hill. The Christmas season glittered and flickered from nearly every home. From a property owner outlining his entire house, tree, and fence in lights, to a simple tree placed in the front window. Lit cutouts of snowmen, reindeer, and Santa seated in his sleigh decorated yards. Nativity scenes gave passersby a reminder of the reason to celebrate.

I was about to take a left onto Willow Drive, when I noticed a gray figure standing in front of the living room window of the corner house. Peeping Tom? Burglar staking out the inside?

I parked near the curb, exited, and opened my trench coat for easy access to my .380. The person either hadn't noticed me or didn't care. At the edge of the lawn, I halted and called out.

"Hey, what's going on?"

"Shh!" was the rely. "Stay quiet or they'll hear you."

"Who are you? What are you doing?"

"Watching my wife and kids put up the Christmas tree."

I stepped closer.

"Who are you," I repeated.

"Name's Paul Sachs."

In the dim illumination from street lights and the ambient city lights, I saw he stood four inches taller than me. He wore jeans and a nylon winter coat. Its hood was down exposing his sandy haired head. His hands were in the coat's pockets, which made me wary.

"Let's see your hands," I said.

He smiled and showed me he carried nothing.

"Answer my second question. What are you doing?"

"As I said, I'm watching my family decorate for Christmas."

Something about the man's attitude and demeanor diminished my anxiety. I didn't know how to explain it, but I received no bad vibes, no aura of enmity. Instead, a sense of calm radiated from him. The closer I walked, the more at ease I felt. Maintaining a safe distance, I peered into the front window. The living room was if small with a recliner, two-cushion sofa, and a Christmas tree that reached almost to the ceiling.

A woman in her middle thirties, dressed in a sweater and jeans stood on a short wooden stool and draped a string of silver tinsel over the branches. A boy, maybe eight years old, hung a simple round gold colored ornament on a low branch. He then scampered back to the sofa and an open box and selected another ornament, a red gowned angel complete with wings and harp. He held it up and I heard his question through the slit in the opened window.

"Where shall I put his one, mommy?"

The woman looked at him. "That's one of Sarah's projects from last year. Let's hang it in the middle of the tree.

With one hand she held the tinsel and with the other reached down, accepted the ornament, and placed the hook over the end of a mid level branch.

I turned my attention back to Sachs.

"Why don't you go in and help?"

He drew a long breath, let it out in a slow ten second release. "I...can't do that. It wouldn't be right."

"I don't understand."

He met my stare.

"I left them almost a year ago."

"I see. And now you're back? To stay or only for a short visit?"

"No, I couldn't stay."

The woman had looped the tinsel almost to the bottom of the tree. The boy had another ornament in hand, waiting.

"It's Christmas," I said. "I don't know the reason you went away, but surely you could work it out."

Sachs shook his head. "No. It's not possible."

"Why?"

"Oh, look," he said and pointed inside. "There's Sarah."

A girl, who looked to be a year away from being a teenager had stepped into the living room. She had a blonde ponytail and bright green eyes. Both hands held a square box perhaps the size of an inexpensive gift box seen at the dollar stores. She carried the box out in front of her, almost with reverence.

"I've brought the star, Mom."

"That's wonderful. Put it on the end table and we'll put it up last."

Sarah gently placed the box on the table and removed the lid. She looked inside for a long moment, then walked to the sofa and plucked up silver ball with a metal lop on top for the hook. By turns, she and her brother, and mother hung ornaments.

"Sarah and Daniel," Sachs said, his voice soft. "The two best accomplishments I ever had in my life."

"They look like great kids," I said.

"Yeah." He gave a short laugh. "Well, it's all their mother's fault. I mean, we both worked hard to raise them properly, but Amy was truly my better half."

"So, up until last year, everything was all right."

"Oh, sure. We both had successful careers, took the kids for weekend trips, vacations, you know, all the traditional family events. Sarah played softball. Daniel plays piano like a savant."

I buttoned and tied the trench coat, but realized, that though the temperature couldn't be over twenty, the cold hadn't affected me. I wasn't campfire warm, but I don't think I had shivered once in the last five minutes.

"Help me understand," I said. "It sounds like you had a...well, forgive the holiday reference, wonderful life. Why would you leave? Haven't you missed them this past year?"

His eyes narrowed and his voice dropped low. "Of course I've missed my family. I'm not heartless."

"Why then-"

Sachs interrupted me. "I think they're almost finished."

I looked and indeed, the tree was covered with ornaments. Someone had plugged in the lights and sparkles of color shone from the branches.

Amy, Daniel, and Sarah stood back and faced the tree. "It's beautiful," Amy said and held her children close.

"Mom," Sarah said. "Do you...think Dad would have liked it?"

"I know he would, honey."

"I wish he could be here," her brother said.

"We all do."

"Why did he have to go?"

"I don't know," Amy said. "Come and sit with me a moment."

She led them to the sofa, set aside the ornament boxes, and sat. Daniel and Sarah knelt before her.

"Listen, you two. Last year, Christmas was rough for all of us. Your father was gone, but we stuck together and survived. During this last year, we all worked hard to live without him, to take strength and support from each other. It's been tough and there have been times when money was tight. But the bills were paid, we never went without food, and we managed to put away a little extra in reserve."

"Daddy taught us how to do that, right?" Daniel asked.

"Yes, he did. I think we owe a lot to him, even though he can't be here."

"What about the star?" Daniel asked.

Amy nodded. "Yes. We won't forget that."

Sarah stood and from the box on the end table, withdrew a five pointed gold colored star. One of the points became the hollow base for the ornament. I saw it had been fashioned to be placed over the top vertical branch of the tree.

Amy and Daniel stood near Sarah as she held the star in her hands. From my vantage point, I saw that there was an insert in the middle that held two photographs.

A picture of Jesus next to a picture of Sachs.

"Turn it on, Mommy," Daniel said, "and put it on the tree."

Amy flicked a small switch on the base and tiny lights around the picture lit up. She repositioned the stool in front of the tree, stepped up and placed the star over the top branch.

Beside me, I heard Sachs whisper, "It's time for me to go. Merry Christmas, Mallory."

I didn't respond, mesmerized by the scene before me. Mother, son, and daughter in front of the tree that was topped with an image of the man they missed along with the Lord.

"Do you think Daddy's watching us, Mommy?" Daniel said.

Amy nodded. "Yes. I believe he's up there with Jesus watching everything we do. I also think that though he would like to be here with us, he's very happy for us."

My eyes widened when I realized what she meant. I whipped around to face Sachs...who had disappeared.

How? And how did he know my name?

Then something quickened my heart rate even more. When I scanned the yard, mine were the only tracks in the snow.

Terri Duncan

Terri is a cancer survivor who wanted to donate a message to everyone who's going through cancer and who have fought it. Terri lives in Pella and loves working with people. She has written several poems and short stories for fun. She loves her family a lot especially her four grandchildren.

Missy Mouse

Little Missy Mouse says hello. She wants you to know that she is thinking about you and praying for you every day.

She knows that you are sick and feeling bad, that you have

to take medicine to get better. Missy knows that you have to see a lot of doctors and nurses. Big machines, little machines. Needles and pills

She Also knows that some days you just don't feel like talking. Sometimes all you want to do is cry. That some days you feel like eating and some days you don't

Missy says you'll have days that you don't want anyone around. There will be days you don't want to be alone.

Good days, bad days, Bad days and good days. Up and down days. Laughing days and crying days.

Missy says she loves you and feels your pain. Because, you see, Missy had cancer and went through all you are going through.

She says never give up. Keep on going. Laugh all you can. Because she says laughter is the best medicine, not only for you, but for others as well.

You are in my prayers every day.

Love Missy Mouse

Linzie Salmons

Linzie is a 34 years old socially inept super klutz that still hasn't figured out what he wants to be when he grows up who lives with best friend, a Black Lab named Princess Dashing. He writes mostly poetry and especially likes poems focusing on deep emotion.

Love

The moment I looked into thine, eyes of a bluest blue the summer skies.

My heart did catch up in my throat.

I was lost at once there is no hope.

With wisdom and wit a razor's edge.

You cut my soul from out its hedge.

A beauty lost within her mind.

A wandering soul from another time.

Sorrow and misery are soon left behind.

You flew through me like a mid-winters wind.

My body and mind I bend to thine whim.

Aphrodite Athena Artimus to a goddess of beauty and love I truly name you.

Dream of her

As I strolled through city fair

I happened to glance a maiden there

A smile so bright the sun did swoon

Eyes did outshine the fullest moon

A laugh to make the lark weep in remorse

It felt vulgar empty and course

She was the dawn

So blessed so clean

Alas your name to me is queen

To know you would be heaven's delight

Yet there you are every night

Was it real was it dream

Perchance to know was both it seems

To dance upon this foolish flight

Faeish dear the world set right

To know your voice and endless grace

My life I would give for your lips just a taste

To feel the touch of divine fingertips

Ah it was a dream realities slip

Return the day of darkness so soon

I wait eagerly the return of the moon

A Dream

Smiling eye's of emerald green

A floating laugh perchance it seems

Hither yonder ecstasy screams

Such lucid thoughts of sacred themes

Flight of fancy no going back

Heart aflutter without much slack

Hopeless roaming within is seems

All of this a fantastic dream

Remembered

A laugh

A smile

A tear

A frown

Daily I see you standing out of the crowd

To know your voice and touch of your lips

To feel until death your fingertips

A soul burned hollow

A mind torn asunder

Your memory to me echoes like thunder

Without the tears, here to remind

Never again you by my side

I sit alone waiting and knowing

You are in my heart always remembered

Untitled

Through a darkened rift I walk alone

A life adrift a soul alone

To yonder shores, I set my sail

With all the strife within this hell

Miserable and broken

To Valhalla's walls

The sands of time around me fall's

Severed and bloody to your door I crawl

Bleached white stone tainted red from crimson falls

With a knock and beat, I do call

Yet with silence do meet such harsh pinfall's

Love was there a moment ago

Where is it now to where did it go?

Painful numbness it does creep

From the top of my head to the soles of my feet

To whence did all such goodness go?

Was it ever there or bare like stone

Shall I wait for tomorrow's dawn

Or shall I pass this life agone?

Lee Collins

Lee Collins is a retired teacher, now a writer. She was educated at The College

of Wooster in Ohio, the University of Pittsburgh, and Rutgers University. She has taught in seven different states, eleven school districts and all grades from kindergarten to college. Her debut novel, published in 2013, TOO MUCH LEFT UNSAID, covers several generation of

the Connors family, especially as they survived the 1960s.

Learn more about Lee at:

Amazon.com - To Much Left Unsaid

This Star Won't Go Out

Sally wanted to get the tree decorated while Lillie was sleeping. Her slim hands trembled as she reached into the cardboard box and pulled out the few homemade decorations and a string of multiple-colored lights. She thought about her sailor husband, Jack, who was serving in Korea. Before he left, he promised to be home for Christmas, "if only in my dreams." And though peace talks were underway in Panmunjom, the evening news was not optimistic that the conflict would end anytime soon. There at the bottom of the box lay the beautiful star, their "Marshall Field's" star. She lifted it out and held it up to admire as she thought of Jack. She was remembering the previous Christmas, their first, when she and Jack had bought it. Her brown eyes filled with tears and yet a smile graced her face as she thought of Jack, away in the service. Their eight-month-old daughter Lillie, sighed in her sleep and stirred a bit in the crib crowded into the corner of their studio apartment. One simple room, with a small kitchenette behind a screen, was furnished with only a sofa bed, a dresser, Lillie's crib, a gate-legged table and two chairs, and the coffee table. The little pine tree that Sally had found in the alley by the school stood on that table waiting to be trimmed.

A year before, Sally and Jack had had no tree. They decorated their floor lamp as a substitute tree with paper streamers and the homemade decorations. They spent Christmas Day, 1950, in this Chicago apartment, near Great Lakes Naval Training Station where Jack was based. Their resources were slim. Sally had cut up magazine pictures and pasted them on colored paper to decorate. She had made paper chains and trimmed the few cards she had received from her Iowa friends into holiday shapes. She and Jack promised each other an after-Christmas trip to the Chicago Loop to admire the holiday decorations, especially the ones at Marshall Field and Company, the twelve-story department store stretching from State Street to Wabash, Randolph to Washington downtown.

The morning after Christmas, they took the "el" to the Loop. Jack was handsome in his Navy blues and Sally glowed in her Sears Roebuck maternity top, navy blue with a white sailor collar. They strolled the entire block around the building, enjoying the windows filled with Christmas goodies and décor. Then they took each other's hands, entered the store and wandered the Marshall Field's building from top to bottom. At each level they admired anew the store's enormous Christmas tree, reaching up under the Tiffany Dome where over a million pieces of glass were used in the large glass mosaic ceiling.

They exclaimed over the elegance and radiance of the many festive displays throughout the store as they rode escalators and wandered aisles. They ended up in the basement Christmas shop where sales were in progress. Sally caught her breath when she saw the glorious eight-pointed star made of silver-colored filigree. Ten inches tall, it seemed to reflect the very star that shone over Bethlehem when the baby born to save mankind was laid in a manger and the angels declared to the shepherds in the field, "Glory to God in the highest, and on earth Peace." The star ornament was still expensive at 60 percent off, but it and a single string of lights would be the perfect touch, the frosting on the cake of that wonderful newlywed Christmas.

"Jack, there are still eleven more days of Christmas! Let's buy this star and hang it on the lamp to enjoy the remaining days. If we buy it, I promise I'll stretch our food budget to make up for it. "

So, it was done. They enjoyed their star until the Christmas holiday ended and it was time to pack up the decorations. When they did so, it seemed as if they were packing their dreams away.

Lillie's birth in April was difficult, the more so since Jack had already been deployed. Lillie was a fussy baby for the first seven months, and was only now beginning to sleep through the night with few interruptions.

But this Christmas there was this little tree, found outside the school which the janitors had thrown out when Christmas break began. Now, as Sally sat and unwrapped the decorations it was like unwrapping the packed-away dream. The magazine-picture decorations, the scissored-Christmas cards looked almost pathetic on the scavenged tree. Still, those decorations represented their first Christmas together.

Sally's vision blurred with tears, as she brought out the Marshall Field's Star. She strung the lights. She hung the homemade ornaments. She draped the chains of colored paper. And lovingly she placed her Marshall Field's star on the top of the modest tree. The star shone as a symbol of Christmas and of her love for Jack. And it was a promise, too, of the gifts of God's love. She heard Lillie's intermittent whimpers, crooned *Silent Night* to her as she plugged in the tree. She turned off the room lights, walked over to the crib, and gently lifted her child.

Lillie pointed at the sparkling lights on the tree and her eyes widened. The lights were reflected in the window, the mirror and in her mother's eyes. Sally looked around and remembered the Field's tree that had so enchanted her and Jack last year. Jack may be here only in his dreams, but they were dreams that the two of them shared, and now Lillie was here to comfort her mother. "And on earth Peace, Little One. Peace will come and Daddy will be

home, Lilliebelle," she whispered. "Merry Christmas."

Rae Hughes

Rae is a founder of the South Central Iowa Paranormal Investigative Team, but when she's not performing investigations she's focusing on her poetry or family. Rae has been a poet for many years and had several poems published in anthologies. She is currently publishing her collection with Makin Books. She is also expecting her first granddaughter.

Learn more about Rae at:

scipit.com

Nature

Come to me, my gentle friends, and travel down the paths of one of life's greatest mysteries. Nature.

It is a warm spring day when all is fresh and new. The sun has just cleared the horizon and the flowers, peeking through the ground, are covered with early morning dew.

We start out this day by taking a walk down a quiet lane, through the trees with their bows beckoning down toward you, showing off their royal majesty.

The air is crisp and clear and you could never feel more vibrant and alive than you do right now, passing amongst all of mother nature's creations without a trace of modern technology anywhere around.

As we look up toward the sky we can see puffs of clouds floating along the breeze. In and out of the clouds the birds dance to the melodies of the animals in the forest.

You thought when we started that it would be quiet, but it is never quiet as long as there is life all around.

There is no need to hurry so just slow down and take time to look everywhere and see all that you can see.

What's that you say? There is nothing to look at? Well you are quite mistaken. Look at the ground and what do you see? Ants, beetles, worms? You might think that you've seen it all before, but guaranteed if you look close enough you'll soon see that each tiny creature has its own characteristics. Take a look at that poor little ant that you about stepped on. Did you realize that he is missing one of his legs and is still trying to carry a heavy load of food home for the others? Or what about that beetle? Can't you see that has only one wing? Even that worm has something different about him. Can you tell what it is?

I'll tell you what it is. You were so blind that you didn't even stop to realize that it isn't even a worm at all, but that it is a caterpillar.

Look up above your head. There's a cocoon that's waiting to hatch. What's in it? Could it be a grand Monarch butterfly or is it just an ordinary butterfly? We can't tell yet.

Let's continue our walk and see what else nature has in store for us.

Spring is the time of birth and new things to be found. It's a time when animals pair up for mating. It's a time when newborn babies are brought into this big world.

As we crest this hill quietly pee in the thick of bushes to your right.

What of all things could be there but two newborn fawns nursing while their mother cleans their young and tender hides. Oh, look, one is trying to stand up. Its little legs are still so wobbly that it just fell right back down. But that doesn't stop it, up it goes again, and this time it manages to take two steps. Can't you feel the mothers pride at having given birth to healthy babies. Although the sight is enough to move you to tears because of how wonderful it is, we must leave them alone for now.

Up ahead the forest gives way to a spacious meadow filled with tall grass and colorful wild flowers. Growing right alongside the trail is the first blossoms of lilies of the valley and blue bells. Just beyond mixed in with the grass are many daisies and a couple scattered lilac bushes.

Standing still you can smell the fragrance of the bushes and the aroma of all the various flowers swaying in the breeze. Some are sweet smelling and some are rather repugnant to the nose.

Hiding in the grass is a tiny little prairie dog, dodging in and out of his hole in the ground. His fur is shedding the last of his winter coat and the dark brown specks are starting to peek through the tan and golden blond fur.

Over in the swampy area of the meadow there are many birds enjoying their daily bath. There are geese heading home after the winter and many gulls feasting on the young fish.

Right by the edge of the water if you are lucky enough you may see a young lion cub trying to take his first swim. First he dips in his right paw then yanks it out real fast, so he tries it with his left paw but decides that it wasn't quite enough so he jumps in with all fours. Needless to say, he didn't stay in very long. He jumps right bac out and quickly goes to find his mama.

Slowly but surely we come out of the meadow and climb up the highest hill around. From there you can see for miles around in every direction. Behind you is the forest and meadow you just left. To your left is the continuous line of hills. To your right is a deep valley filled with all sorts of commotion and wildlife. And ahead of you is the combination of everything, with mountains perching on the horizon line beckoning for you to adventure farther on your walk.

But then you come back to the modern world and see your car coming up the only road there is. It is time to leave for now but soon we can go on another journey.

As we leave this land of peace, solitude, and mysteries, we thank nature for sharing some of its most precious scenes with us and ask it to allow us to come back some day and experience more.

The Waterfall

Round and round the river flows,

Up the hill then down it goes.

Around the bend, and under the bridge,

And then it hits the swirling ground.

It beckons you with words unsaid,

And yet you hear it in your head,

On it goes to an unknown place,

Challenging you to a fast paced race.

Then finally its end it sees,

Approaching silently like a breeze.

Up ahead the waterfall roars,

Come on, it says, it's time for more.

The river flies into midair,

And replies to the waterfall, "Catch me if you dare."

The waterfall reaches and pulls the river down,

The river now makes no sound.

So calling out its victory,

The waterfall say, "I AM KING!"

Antonia Robinson

Antonia was born on the east coast of New Zealand in the small town of Gisborne. In 2010 she went to radio broadcasting school where she enjoyed each moment of it. She later decided to focus full-time on her passions of Art and Writing and recently self-publishing her first poetry book, 'Poems of One's Mind' followed by the sequel 'Poetry for Deeper Thoughts.' 'The Art of Patience' is her third book which won the "Readers Favorite 5 Star Rating Seal"

Learn more about Antonia at:

www.facebook.com/antonia.robinsonauthor

twitter.com/ARobinsonAuthor

Christmas Story

Peace at Christmas, with love on each other's mind

A pocket full of doves, with white snow to clear the mind

Making sense of caroling, and giving on this special day,

Makes you feel at home

Makes you come alive.

You feel like a person when you remember your past

Your family was all around you, there were plenty of photos to take

Plenty of food to indulge in

Plenty of laughs with plenty of delight.

You were told of great stories of Christmas's before yours

And how your mother or father felt

In their childhoods, they could see

The same eyes that you show, and shine.

Same with your grandparents

They had harder times,

Sometimes they didn't have much

And that is why they give you more

That is why they are so in touch.

But Christmas is everywhere

Christmas is every year

You hope to dream of the same as the past

But each Christmas in the future

Turns out different

So the determination of hope at Christmas

And knowing that some have it harder than yourself

Can make you sometimes cry

But also keeps you strong.

Around the world others celebrate

Without a care in the world

With a candle they have in hand

That they call amen.

But others, know the struggles

That some do not process

And present hope in a warm light glow for all

It is truly a blessing in disguise.

Christmas

Peace at Christmas, with love on each other's mind

A pocket full of doves

With white snow to clear the mind.

Making sense of caroling, and giving on this special day,

Makes you feel at home. Makes you come alive.

You feel like a person when you remember your past

Your family was all around you, there were plenty of photos to take

Plenty of food to indulge in

Plenty of laughs with plenty of delight.

You were told of great stories of Christmas's before yours

And how your mother or father felt

In their childhoods they could see

The same eyes that you show, and shine.

Same with your grandparents

They had harder times,

Sometimes they didn't have much

And that is why they give you more

That is why they are so in touch.

But Christmas is everywhere

Christmas is every year

You hope to dream of the same as the past

But each Christmas in the future

Turns out different

So the determination of hope at Christmas

And knowing that some have it harder than yourself

Can make you sometimes cry

But also keeps you strong.

Around the world others celebrate

Without a care in the world

With a candle they have in hand

That they call amen.

But others, know the struggles

That some do not process

And present hope in a warm light glow for all

It is truly a blessing in disguise.

As I Sit In Church

As I sit in a church

Alone and confused,

I remember those times

Where, I did not have to worry

Where, I did not have to forget who I was.

Now I am struggling,

Now I am less than who I am

Weak and confused

Am I too late?

The candles that surround me,

A small but delicate light

It fills me with warmth

They embrace me with hope.

Sheena Macleod

I live in a seaside town in Scotland with my family and two dogs. My basic degree is in Psychology, and I have a Masters in Advanced Mental Health Practice and a PhD from the University of Dundee. A few years ago now, I was diagnosed with lupus, an auto-immune disorder, and retired from my post as a lecturer there to research and write a series of historical fiction novels tracing the lineage of Elizabeth Sutherland; a key person in the Highland Clearances. The first book in this family saga, Reign of the Marionettes, published by Makin Books Publisher, should be available for purchase, early in 2017. I am currently working on the follow up, which continues where the first book leaves off.

An avid reader, writer and beta reader, I try to contribute time and support to the One Million Project, OMP, of which I am a creative member. OMP comprises a group of almost 100 authors and artists who contribute some of their work in an effort to raise 1 million for homelessness and cancer charities.

Lean more about Sheena at:

reignofthemarionettes.wordpress.com

Christmas Cards

Snow-filled clouds gathered outside the high-rise flats. Inside, in a small sitting room on the ninth floor, Janie MacKay's gaze drifted back to the official-looking envelope on the mantelpiece. Sitting beside the letter, a clock mocked her as it ticked off the minutes until the contents came into force. Many others throughout Scotland would have received the same standard letter. The only difference would be the name and address on it, she thought.

Chewing on a fingernail, she wondered what to do. She had grown up in the care system and learned early to let other people make decisions for her. Her mother had died when Janie was two-years-old, and she had no idea who her father was. Having been moved about between foster homes, she had grown up feeling on the periphery of life. Though she was made welcome in these people's homes, she had no recollection of what it felt like to be a 'real' member of a family.

Ten years ago, when she turned sixteen, a social worker had brought her and her meagre possessions to this flat. A sitting area, bedroom, kitchen and bathroom within the large multi-story complex soon became her home. She had been taught to cook, shop and clean. No sooner had she stepped through the door that first day, when a large van arrived with the new 'white goods' and household basics that she was entitled to from the Council; a fridge-freezer, washing machine, cooker, bed, chairs, and more. She had stroked it all, unable to believe her eyes. Every week she received unemployment benefit and, by setting some aside, had saved enough for a second-hand multi-media screen with a built-in social network box.

Janie looked over at the media screen. She recalled the soaps she used to watch, the dramas and sitcoms. She missed them all. Her electricity had been cut off over three months ago. Sometimes she replayed her favorite media programmers in her head.

Janie's attention returned to the mock-mantelpiece, and a distant memory of a similar one filled with Christmas cards flashed before her eyes. Unable to help herself, she lifted the letter down and re-read it. Tomorrow, the 14th December 2036 she would receive her last phased payment of unemployment benefit. The government no longer had the funds to pay benefits of any kind. Arrangements had been put in place to drop off a food parcel to her twice a week. She could remain in her flat, but no services or repairs would be provided.

Janie's low mood deepened. She had been blighted by depression for years; unable to work she had found ways to exist on her own. Though she had had lots of virtual people she chatted to on her social network box, she had no real-time friends who could help her now. With no electricity, she had been unable to log in. She missed her friends from the therapy group, the members of the exercise class, her chat site 'buddies'. At the flick of a switch they had been removed from her life. The pain she felt had been no less acute than if they had all suddenly died. She had grieved for each and every one of them.

These people had seemed real to her then; they had been the center of her life. She had been delighted by each of the virtual birthday and Christmas cards they had sent her. In her mind, she had visualized their hands passing their cards to her in friendship. With no real-time social outlets, they had made life livable. Apart from food shopping, she rarely ventured outside.

Truth hit her like a punch in the chest; she was isolated and lonely, and had been since she moved here. People surrounded her in the numerous flats throughout the complex, but she had never spoken to one of them. Like her, they were unemployed and rarely ventured out, and when they did they kept their heads bowed low.

Sighing, Janie pulled on a warm coat and made her way outside. It was late and starting to get dark. She needed to think, plan what to do. While she walked around the multi-story building, she picked up an armful of twigs. Returning to the front entrance, she sat down and scrunched the letter in her hands. Using a twig, she dug a small hole and placed the letter into the stony ground. She flicked her lighter and lit the paper. Then, she settled twigs on top.

Sitting cross-legged in front of the fire, she started to sing. Gently at first, then her voice rose as it did when she sang along to the social media church. Soon, other people from the complex gathered beside her and joined in the song. Most brought wood for the fire. As their voices filled the air, Janie felt a sense of exhilaration she had never felt before. It was as if her spirit had been set free.

The following evening, they gathered around the fire again and told each other stories; some dramatic, some funny. When soft flurries of snow started to fall, Janie looked up and let the flakes glide onto her face. She couldn't remember the last time it had snowed in December. She wondered if it was a sign; an omen.

Evening after evening, Janie joined the others who gathered around the fire outside their building. Within a week, they had started to meet during the day. Together, they pooled their resources and provided for each other. A group soon formed, to carry out household repairs. Another group set up, to alter, refashion or repair clothes. Janie joined a group who looked after the children; so their parents could work in a particular group. Someone even suggested pooling a small sum of money, to buy seeds to plant in the spring.

As Janie glanced around the smiling faces surrounding her, she realized that these people had become her real-time friends. She could hardly remember any of the virtual people she used to speak to on her social network box. They had been no more real than the virtual Christmas cards they had sent her. Thinking of this made her recall the pens and paper she had in a drawer. She hoped she had enough sheets of paper to make each of her new friends a real Christmas card. She would start making them tomorrow.

On Christmas morning, Janie found an envelope that had been pushed under her door. Brushing back a tear, she opened it and placed her Christmas card onto the mantelpiece. When she joined the others around the fire, she handed out her home-made cards. Later, someone dragged out a fake Christmas tree, and the children decorated it with ribbons made from strips cut from an old sheet.

Sitting around the fire with the others, Janie Mackay looked up at the star-filled sky; a sky filled with hope. A few weeks ago she had grieved for the loss of her virtual friends; never again would she see their light shine. Today, she knew this star would never go out. She recalled what she had read about her ancestors being cleared from their homes and sent to live on the barren cliff-edges in the remote highlands of Scotland. They had survived losing their homes and became stronger in the process, and so would she.

The Christmas Present

Waking to orange peel, pine needles, morning dawning clear

Frost on windows clouding the view of sleighs,

jingling over freshly fallen snow.

Putting on dressing gown, soft slippers, hurrying down stairs

Breakfast first at a table set for eight,

a tradition not to be rushed.

Seeing the filled stockings, colorful parcels, waiting to be explored

Taking turns to give and receive, passing parcels onwards

until finally my turn arrives.

Stilling beating heart, silencing thoughts, no idea what is inside

Filled with hope, ribbon released and paper tossed aside

to reveal the final truth.

Eyes turning, mouth wide, it is just what I wanted.

Teresa Tallman

Teresa Tallman graduated in 1975 from Iowa State University with a degree in Chemical Engineering. She worked for 35 years for a major manufacturing company and is the author of Hear the Word series...Fun with Statistics for toddlers aged 3-5.

Learn more about Teresa at:

Amazon – Fun With Statistics

A Boy Named Jake

Since I had a break in my food bank client interviews I left my office and looked around the food pick up area. Stacked along the walls were perishables. Browning strawberries. Tomatoes. Stacks and Stacks of bread. Box upon box of donuts. I always wondered why the grocery stores made so many extra donuts. We had glazed, cream filled, chocolate coated dusted with sprinkles. And there were always cartons and cartons of ripening bananas. I reminded people that they freeze well and are great in shakes or banana bread.

I spotted a young mother with two children who looked to be about three years old. The little girl wore pink stretchy pants and the little boy was dressed in a plaid shirt, jeans and cowboy boots. The mom was searching through stacks of cookies and desserts. I asked how her day was going and if the children could have a treat. She smiled and agreed.

I found some extra-luscious cupcakes and offered them to the little ones. The girl swept her gold hair back, smiled and took the treat from my hand. The boy took the cupcake from my hand, looked at the floor and gave the treat to the girl. I marveled that the he wasn't swayed by my offering.

I squatted to look them both in the eyes

"What are you names?"

"I'm Emma and this is Jake."

Emma was a gorgeous, obviously happy little girl. The boy was the same age and looked like my grandson but wore soulfulness beyond his years.

"Would you like a book?"

"Yes. Yes." Emma answered.

Little Jake looked at me, but didn't respond. Again, I was struck with the deep look in his eyes. Was it sadness? I had never seen that look on such a young face before. It was almost like he knew that things weren't the best a home. They didn't have enough food. There wasn't enough money and he wasn't comfortable coming somewhere for handouts. Was it possible that an innocent, small child can have that awareness?

Not to be deterred I went to the book case and found a few used, age appropriate books. Again, Emma gladly accepted them, and showed her mom. Jake blandly looked at the books and set his on the chair next to him.

"He's shy." His mom said.

I was intent on getting little Jake to cheer up and realize that the food bank was a friendly place for him to be. I went to the back office and found a few new books about princesses and super heroes. Emma thought it was wonderful and the day must be a holiday. Jake started to break a smile, but a few minutes later I noticed he put that book down also. He caught my eye to say, 'Is that all you've got?'

Determined, I had one last trick up my sleeve. There were a few left over Christmas presents in the back room. I hoped there would be some for a couple 3 year olds. Sure enough, I found a precious doll with flaxen hair that looked like Emma and a big, new red truck that was still in the box.

Jake took the truck and turned it every which way up. He held that truck close to his body the rest of the 20 minute visit. I felt triumphant. I did it. 'Don't mess with a grandma.' I thought.

I finished some filing I had to do. When I returned to pick up area, I didn't see Jake and Emma.

"They just left." Our receptionist told me.

I walked out to the parking lot. I saw Mom, Emma and little Jake about 20 feet away from the building.

"Bye Emma. Bye Jake."

Emma turned and waved big. Jake kept walking, with the truck clutched to his chest. I thought he wasn't going to respond. And then, there it was. He never turned around, but his right hand fell below his hips and he gave me a wave. I was thrilled. The day was a win-win. I felt wonderful and

for one day we gave a little boy a ray of hope. And a truck.

Jacque Leigh

Jacque began writing seriously, after continuing the research her mother started on their ancestors. Her first writing was a group of short stories, compiling a memoir. One; a tale of a family Sunday afternoon drive, was printed in the Des Moines Sunday Register, in a column that featured memories of life in the 1950s.

"Roots Through Time" is her first attempt at a novel, that started as a fiction story of the life of her Great-grandfather and his family.

Jacque is a mother of five and grandmother of nine. She enjoys spending time with all of them and the family gathers several times throughout the year. She has lived most of her life in Iowa, and loves to travel to see other places, where she gathers a lot of her ideas for characters.

She is working on two more novels, but both are just in the beginning stages.

Learn more about Jacque at:

Amazon - Roots Through Time

There's Always Hope

Oneita sat rocking in the rocker that her grandfather had built his wife at the turn of the century nearly thirty-six years ago now. She was sewing a small garment from the fabric recycled from her worn out slip. It was soft from the many washings, therefore perfect for the little gown she was fashioning for the wee one soon to make an appearance. This surprise addition to the family would be their sixth child coming eight years after the last. She rocked back and forth keeping time with the in and out motion of the needle through the cloth. It was late into the evening. The younger two boys had been tucked in for the night and their two teen girls were busy at the table with their homework. The wind howled around the corners of the small house, but the coal stove next to her rocker radiated warmth to all but the furthest corners. She was waiting for her firstborn son and Ray her husband to return from delivering coal to a family at the edge of town. Chances are they would return with empty pockets. Too many times the customer didn't have two pennies to rub together let alone money for coal. Ray was just too kind hearted to push anyone for payment.

"Girls, it's time to put away the books and turn in. Be sure to add an extra quilt to the bed and check to see if the boys have enough to keep them warm."

She heard the rumble of the truck motor and let out a sigh of relief. Her men were home. She plunged the needle into the pincushion and folded the tiny garment into her sewing basket. The rocker continued rocking after she had risen from the seat and walked toward the door to unlock it. It was always a good idea to keep the door locked when the men were away. The small house was located on the lonely windswept prairie miles from any other inhabitants. Many times dilapidated trucks loaded high with household goods drove down their dusty road headed west where they hoped to make a better life. Not every vehicle contained innocent families. You never knew when part of the criminal population would approach. She shivered when she remembered how close Bonnie and Clyde had been to their farm at one time.

Ray and their eldest son entered the house and the wind drove a bucket of snow into the corner of the room. Ray slapped his hands against his arms. His coat was much too thin for this December weather. By morning they could have eight inches of snow piled up outside and a temperature of only five degrees. He really needed a heavy coat. So much of his handyman work was performed outside in the frigid weather. How many times Oneita wished for better clothing for her family. There just wasn't enough money for everything these days.

Christmas was two days away and there was no spare change for gifts. Even though they would have been necessary items for the family. Shoes without holes for the young boys. Warm boots for walking to school for the teen girls and a heavy coat for Ray.

She moved the star shaped lamp to the window in case a needy family was seeking shelter. Under her breath she whispered. "This light with not go out."

***

The next afternoon Ray was returning home from his last delivery. He drove the dump truck across a small creek and noticed a pine tree growing in the ditch. It had a full symmetrical shape an unusual occurrence in ditch trees. He pulled over, exited the truck, located the hand saw in his toolbox and tracked through the drifts, toward the six-foot tree. His foot slipped on the way down into the ditch and that pitched him forward into a three-foot drift. The snow caked around his neck and he felt a chill to his feet. In the struggle to gain footing, Ray's mitten less hands became stiff with cold so it took him twenty minutes to saw through the trunk of the tree. With that task accomplished, he struggled back to the top of the ditch, tossed the tree into the back of the vehicle, and headed on down the road.

***

Oneita reached out her hand to steady herself and walked into the room just in time

to see Ray struggling with a green monster.

"What in the world are you up to now?"

Ray pulled the pine through the door with one last jerk.

"This is our Christmas tree! Isn't it a great one? I found it growing in a ditch down on Hindsville road. Just couldn't pass it up."

"But, Ray, we don't have decorations or gifts to put under it. I wouldn't want the boys to get their hopes up and be disappointed in the morning."

She placed her hand on her stomach and let out a groan.

Ray dropped the tree and rushed to her side.

"Is the baby coming?"

"Yes, I think we are going to have an addition to the family tonight."

Ray wrapped his arm around her back and helped her into the bedroom.

"Here lay down and I'll get Rose to fetch the doctor."

"No, don't bother him on Christmas Eve. I'll be ok. Remember I delivered our last without any help."

Ray shook his head from side to side.

"That was eight years ago. At least let me send for Widow Rodgers."

Oneita rolled from side to side with another contraction.

"That'll be good. I don't want Rose trying to help."

He left her and went to find Rose.

"Rose, could you run next door and ask the Widow Rodgers to come help your mother. Tell her it is time. She'll know what you mean."

"Daddy, I know what that means, and sure I'll go get her."

Ray returned to the kitchen and pondered over the tasks to be done to prepare for Christmas morning.

"We'll need to pop some corn for the boys to string? And find an old catalog for them to cut into snowflakes. They can decorate our tree with those items."

Rose returned with Widow Rodgers and led her to the bedroom where her mother was nearing her delivery time.

"Rose, please boil a pot of water for me and we'll get this delivery underway."

The family scurried to fix things for Christmas and a new baby.

Ray wound the handle on the Victrola in the corner of the room, it rotated a record, and Bing Crosby crooned "Silent Night". The two boys sat at the table cutting away at the colorful pages of the old Sears and Roebuck catalog. Rose pumped water into the large kettle and placed it on the burner of the cook stove next to the pot that her sister shook. The corn in that pan started popping and Rose inhaled the buttery smell, and her mouth watered. The older son brought more wood to create heat for the cook stove, then returned to the basement for a load of coal for the heat stove in the parlor. Ray fashioned a stand from planks of wood for the tree, then stood it in the empty corner nearest the large window. With that finished, he headed up the ladder to the attic. He knew just the item for the top of the tree. It was up here somewhere.

When he returned to the room, there was pounding on the door. He dropped the item in his hand onto the table and went to see who was calling on them on Christmas Eve.

"Oh, hello Viktor, what brings you out on this night? Do you need more coal?"

Viktor Ivanov pushed a box toward Ray.

"No, Mr. Bonne', I bring gift for family."

"Bu- But why? You don't owe us anything"

"You be good man to my family. We leave in morning for Texas. We'll live with my brother, where it's warm. We won't need these."

He proceeded to pull items from the box.

"Here's boots for your girls. See fur the inside will keep their feet warm and these are good leather shoes for your boys. They no longer fit my boys. He then pulled out a bear skin coat this is for you, and last a pretty dress for your wife. My Sylvia is now too fat for them."

He turned before Ray could refuse the gifts and disappeared into the night.

A baby's cry from the bedroom distracted Ray and he shoved the box into the hall closet and made his way to the bedroom.

Widow Rodgers was placing a small blanket covered bundle into Oneita's arms. She turned when he entered the room and said,

"Come in and meet your new daughter. I understand her name is to be Jeanne?"

He tiptoed to the side of the bed and bent down to kiss first his exhausted wife then the damp head of his baby girl.

"This is going to be one spoiled little lassie. Her older sisters will treat her like a favorite doll."

Oneita patted his hand.

"I imagine you'll do your share of spoiling too."

Ray laughed from way down in his belly.

"You know me too well. On another note. You'll be surprised in the morning, and that's all I'm going to say for now. Get your rest. The boys have decorated the tree and gone to bed. The girls are finishing up in the kitchen and will soon follow them."

He led Widow Rodgers to the door where Rose was waiting to walk her home.

"Rose do you have that cooked dish for her?"

"Yes, Daddy, here it is; I'll carry it for her."

"Ok, hurry back so we can settle in for the night."

He turned his attention to the item he had left on the table. It was golden in color and twinkled as the light reflected off it. He reached to the top of the tree and placed there the star his mother had put at the top of their tree when he was a boy. That job finished he pulled the box from the closet and using last month's newspapers, he wrapped each item and wrote a name on the package as tears flowed down his cheeks. Miracles do happen he decided.

Rose returned and the two of them gazed at the transformed tree. The star at the top twinkled even though there was no other light in the room. Rose smiled at the sight.

"This light will not go out."

Carol Clarke Reed

I have two adult children, a son and a daughter. When my daughter was young, she donated her long brown hair to "Locks of Love". My world has been effected by several family members fighting different types of cancer.

I have an Associate of Applied Science and an Associate of Arts.

I have a short story published in the Flagler IA Area History, 1877 - 1998. A poem published, in Poetic Voices of America, fall 1994 and another in Nature's Gentle Kiss, "The International Library of Poetry." My third published poem in a poetic book, which was also listed in Poetry.com. I have short stories published on CDs through the Annual Iowa Summer Writing Festival. I've also been known to express my opinion through Letters to the Editor. I have written several articles for Hub.pages.com.

I have experienced the world of Acting, under the same pen name.

I'm a member of the Marion County Writer's Workshop in Knoxville, Iowa and I've attended several of the Iowa Summer Writing Workshops.

Learn more about Carol at:

hubpages.com/@carolreed

Charismatic Cassey

Once upon a time, on Christmas Eve, when time stood still for every child in the hospital. A white-haired man with a long white beard met a little girl with no hair. His jolly round body, covered with a red velvety and white fluffy suite, wobbled like a penguin into her room.

"Ho. Ho. Ho, sweet little charismatic Cassey. Merry Christmas! Have you thought about what you would you like for Christmas, besides getting unhooked from all these machines, not being woke up during the night for blood work and being able to go home?"

Cassey's bright smile and low voice confessed, "Yes, I would like hair like yours." She smiled.

"Ho.Ho.Ho. I will tell you what I will do."

Cassey's frail body sat up as straight as she could.

"Close your eyes dear girl and count to three before you open them again."

"One, two, three," she said in a whisper, before opening her eyes. Cassey let out an, "Oh," before she covered her mouth in surprise at what she was looking at."

"Ho.Ho.Ho…What's wrong dear girl?"

"What happened to your hair, Santa?"

He handed her a mirror and said, "Ho. Ho. Ho. What do you mean, Charismatic Cassey?"

She scratched her head and said, "Wha… Oh my…" and then she burst out in laughter and played with the white curls hanging from the top of her head, dangling over her shoulders and down her back. She laughed so loud that she drew an audience of nurses, doctors and other children that called the hospital their home.

"Ho. Ho. Ho. Charismatic Cassey. Do I not look like Santa?"

Now holding both hands to her own mouth, she snickered, "NO."

The others in the room were standing with mouths open, eyebrows raised and whispering.

"Do I sound like Santa?"

"Yes."

"Look at my face. Does my face look like me?"

"Yes, but without your hair." She snickered.

"Look in the mirror. Do you look like you?"

"No," she giggled.

The people standing in the room were silent. By this time, there wasn't any space for another hallway passerby. Her mom sat beside Cassey with both hands on her bed, listening to the conversation between her daughter and the jolly man in red. Cassey's parents took shifts in staying overnight with her and this was Cassey's dad's night home.

"Do you sound like you," Santa continued.

"Yes." She chuckled.

"Do you know why I call you Charismatic Cassey?"

She shook her head and said, "No," and then brought the glistening white hair to her nose, she said, "Do you know your hair smells like sugar cookies?"

A tear ran down her mom's cheek as she said, "Honey you can smell sugar cookies?"

The people in the room smiled.

"And it makes me hungry," Cassey said.

Another tear ran down her mom's cheek. "I've waited a long time to hear you say that you're hungry."

One of the nurses said," I'll get right on that," before exiting the room.

"Sorry, Santa, but why do you call me Charismatic Cassey?"

"Ho.Ho.Ho. Because you are like a magnet. Your charisma, which is charm or your spirit is full of life. Look around this room, you have a talent for attracting people to you."

"Ha. ha. he. he." She leaned toward Santa. "I don't think they are here to see me, I think they are here to see you," Cassey said. She looked around the room and watched each on shake their head from side to side.

"You're here to see me?"

They all nodded.

Santa pulled an empty chair up to the side of her bed. He sat down and said," Cassey, it isn't what is on the outside that makes a person. It's what is on the inside. 'Beauty is a beauty does.' You have a wonderful inside and people see this in you. Younger children look up to you and by the looks of these people in your room, the older look up to you also. Now close your eyes and count to three, but this time…" He looked around the room. "I need all of you to close your eyes too. Ho.ho.ho. No peaking Troy, you are still on the good list." He turned back to Cassey and nodded.

"One, two, three." She opened her eyes. Santa was no longer bald. Cassey looked in the mirror and smiled. I am who I am, inside and out.

The people in the room, left one at a time and as they left they said, "Good-night Charismatic Cassey."

Before Santa left the room, he kissed Cassey on the forehead, shook her mom's hand and then said, Goodnight and Merry Christmas.

The nurse returned with a late-night snack of ice cream and a sugar cookie.

The next morning, Cassey woke up and saw a package that Santa had left behind. She unwrapped the gift to find a wig that looked just like her hair before she lost it. She found a note that said, this is a gift from a special girl that had plenty of extra hair and wanted to share her hair with another little girl that would take good care of it. Cassey, held the hair up to show her mom and said," I really don't need it but someone cared enough to share with me so I will wear it proud."

Cassey's father showed up just in time to wheel her down the hallway toward the outside doors.

"Let's get out of here Hot Rod," he said.

"Dad, can we change our tradition to let's get out of here, Charismatic Cassey," she said.

With a smile, Cassey's mom said, "I'll tell you later."

Cassey wore her smile and her new hair in honor as she passed the nurses, doctors and some of the children that stood in the hallway's telling her bye even when she saw a sad little boy at the doorway, sitting in his wheel chair.

"Stop dad."

Her dad brought her chair to a sudden stop.

"Hi," she said

Not making eye contact, he said "Hi."

"Did anyone ever tell you that you have the most beautiful eyes," she said.

He looked at her. His face became red with embarrassment and then smiled.

"There it is. I knew there was a smile inside you," she said.

She tapped her wheelchair with her hand and said," Ok, dad. My job is done here. I'm ready to go home."

Ashley Lovell

Ashley Lovell was born in Pella IA, but raised in Knoxville IA. She grew up living out in the country with her step dad, her mom, and her older brother and sister. They had 5 dogs and 15 cats running around the property. In the summer of 2004 at the age of 16 she thought of her first short story idea, House of Treasures. Ever since then she been writing. She has written poems, short stories and song lyrics in the past.

Back in March of 2007 through March of 2008 she was presented with certificates of outstanding work by Potery.com

Ashley also has a thing for black cats. Spook has been Ashley's writing buddy since 2008 and she also adopted Batman in August of 2016. Batman sits on her lap while she writes and he also sleeps by her head or by her feet at night.

Ashley has serval other different genres of books in the works right now, but none ready to be published yet.

Learn more about Ashley at:

ashleylovell5.wordpress.com

www.facebook.com/ashleylovellebookauthor

Christmas with the McGala's

Alivia woke up to the smell of gingerbread cookies fresh baked from the oven. She set up in bed and looked out the window.

White orbs of snow floated down past the deck onto the rails, chairs, and table.

A layer of snow covered the front yard. Tree branches weighted with patches of snow.

Alivia pulled the covers off and hurried downstairs.

Her mom, sister Fern and Grandpa Quinn were in the living room.

"Morning, Alivia," Grandpa Quinn said.

There was a knock at the door.

Alivia's mom got up and answered it. It was the rest of the family.

"Cuzy's."

Lauretta and Skeeter had some presents in their hands.

"Hi cuzy," Lauretta said holding up the presents.

"My cuzy's are here." Alivia hugged them, so glad they were there with her.

The bottom of the tree was full of different sized boxes. Lights wrapped around the tree and on top was a star.

"Merry Christmas little sister," Fern held a bag up.

"Morning everyone," Alivia said. She gave everyone a hug, including grandpa Quinn. "Morning grandpa."

"Morning, did you sleep well?"

"Yes."

Alivia pulled out the paper in the bag and saw a brand new pair of boots.

"Wow, thanks, Fern."

Alivia hugged her then tried them on. Her foot touched the tipped of the steal. They were the perfect size and they felt great on the inside.

It felt good for the family to get together on Christmas morning. The happiness and joy that Alivia felt filled her heart with love. Seeing everyone smile and laugh made it a good Christmas.

"Okay everyone.," Alivia's mom said. "Time to light the candles." She passed around matches to everyone.

On the shelf were candles that everyone had made years ago. Every year around Christmas the family lights the candles for family members and friends that could not be with them.

Alivia walked over to her candles that was next to grandpas.

"Let's say a prayer."

"In our heavenly farther, guide us, love us on your path. Keep us safe and happy this year. I know you are with our loved ones that can't be with us. In our fathers name, amen."

Alivia lit the match and lit the candle as the others did.

As the candles grew bright she stepped back and knew the light won't go out in her heart.

Cassandra DenHartog

Cassandra is a Physical Therapy Assistant, Massage Therapist, and romance author. She works in a small hospital by day. At night she works on her books and blog. She's a lover of chickens and cute things. She also is a Frontier Head with the Iowa Pokemon Battle Frontier.

Learn more about Cassy at:

www.cassandradenhartog.com

www.facebook.com/CassandraDenHartog

Amazon – Past in Shadows

Vampire's First Christmas

Nikolai looked up in time to see Ada sadly staring at the corner of his apartment. She crossed her hands over her bright green tunic and turned her now dull green eyes to the window.

"What's wrong, my dear?"

She let a soft sigh. "I just…" She trained off.

Nikolai moved up behind her and began to gently knee the knotted muscles of her neck, being careful of his vampire strength. "If there is something wrong I want you to tell me."

She made a soft purr sounds and her head lulled to the side. "It's almost Christmas…."

"And you want to have a tree??"

She nodded slowly. "Or something. I've never…"

His chest tightened. "You've never had a Christmas, have you?"

"We never had holidays…"

Her body tensed. She'd been a forced to do a lot of things she didn't want to by many bad people ever since she was a child. So hurt, but so strong. He hadn't celebrated a holiday in years. Twenty? Maybe forty? "We can celebrate," he whispered in her ear.

She turned and looked up into his eyes. "We can?"

"Yes. Is you trach me."

"Teach you?"

"I haven't celebrated a holiday in even longer than you. Right now, you're the expert."

A smile crossed her rosy lips and the spark returned to her eyes. "Well I guess I can." She eyes the floor for a moment as if thinking. "It's hard to remember back that far."

He chuckled. "You're telling me."

A blush covered her pale cheeks. "Yes. Yes. I remember stringing popcorn. That would be fun." She took a large breath and licked her lips. "I love buttered popcorn."

He frowned and looked towards his kitchen. "I… I might have something." As a vampire, food wasn't a priority. If he found it, would it even be edible anymore? *I need to try for her.* "Let's look."

The two went off to the kitchen and pulled open every cupboard, drawer, cubby, pantry, and even rummaged through the fridge. No popcorn.

Her shoulders slumped. "That's ok."

"Wait." He had to come up with something. He couldn't see her sad, not before Christmas. Their first Christmas, he realized. Nikolai looked at the open rooms. *What would mimic popcorn?* He ran to his desk and pulled out a box of tissues. "If we stitch these together they'll look prettier than popcorn."

She lifted a brow.

"Trust me."

She didn't seem confident, but after twenty minutes of running a needle and thread through tissues they had a string that looked like fluffy snowflakes. He hung it above the window.

After a long while she grinned. "They do look like snowflakes."

He hugged her from behind. "Told you. So what's next?"

"Well… I always wanted to learn how to make paper snowflakes."

He pulled back. He'd never done anything artsy like that before. Did he even own scissors? He did have his sword, but that wouldn't work. *I have to do this for her.*

"What's wrong?"

"Nothing. Let's find some scissors and paper." He paused at his desk, embarrassed at the mess. CDs coated the wood and several lay on the floor. An old coffee cup sat on the empty printer. Papers overflowed from the trash can, half melted from another cup of spilt coffee laying on top of them. He'd been so busy hunting vampires he forgot to do anything with his house. He gave her a sideways glance to see what she thought. She didn't seem to mind, but if she did her expression didn't give her away. "I'll... I'll look for paper." After a few minutes, it became obvious he had no new paper unless receipts counted. *I think they're too small.*

She lifted a pair of scissors. "Found them. Do you have paper?"

He flinched. How could he not have paper? *Who doesn't have paper?* The light in her eyes began to fade. He could not have that. "Wait. Just wait." He had to have something. Anything. But how big were snowflakes? Did it have to be paper sized? *Yes. Maybe?* Cd covers weren't big enough.

"It's ok if we can't do any snowflakes."

"No. No. I'm sure I have something." He reached up and pulled a copy of This Light Won't Go Out from the bookshelf.

"What's that for?"

"Snowflakes."

"Don't ruin a book for that."

He pulled back. "Ruin?" He looked at the old book, well read in its day, but lately he had not touched it. "Choosing a priority is not ruining something. We can use the pages to make something beautiful."

"But the book?"

"Is only an object." He grinned. "You are more important."

Her eyes softened and her body melted a little.

He tore a page from the book and slipped up beside her. "So what am I doing with this now?" He rubbed his face up against hers, giving her a playful cuddle.

She laughed as she pushed him off. "Ok. Ok. I have to look up how to make these." She pulled out her phone and began to search different patterns.

He took the moment to pull his phone out and send a quick text. She found several patterns and they tried them all. He managed to make a blob and something like a spider web. She ripped one and in frustration threw it. The wad of paper hit him in the face.

"Oops."

He gave her a grin, wadded his blob of a snowflake attempt, and threw it at her arm. It was on. The sound of tearing paper and laughter filled the apartment. They waged a snowball like fight with wads of paper diving for more when they ran out. He used his vampire like speed to rush out, grab arm fulls, and duck behind a chair.

"That's cheating!" She charged over and pelted him, one after another, with pieces of paper.

When she ran out he scooped her into his arms and pulled her close. Her warm living body melted him. "What's next."

As her mouth opened her stomach growled.

He laughed, placing a gentle kiss on her head. "I guess food. What's a good holiday food?"

"Cookies would be nice."

He still didn't have a crumb of good food, but he wasn't going to stop now. He'd do anything for her. He didn't have a cookie mix, but remember a cake mix from earlier. He pulled down the yellow cake box and blew the dust off the top. "It's not expired yet."

She took his hand and turned the book so she could read that back. "But I know we don't have milk or eggs. I don't think we can make this."

"Nonsense. There has to be some way to make this into something." He pulled up his phone and read a quick message.

"What is it?"

He shrugged. "Nothing." His thumb traced over the screen. "Here it is. You can use soda instead of eggs."

"No way!" She tried to grab his phone from him.

He yanked back and held it up out of her reach. "I'm not lying. And we have Pepsi."

"For cookies?"

"I'm sure it will work." He gathered a bowel, blowing the dust off first, and mixed the dough together. He ran his finger over the bowel and stuck it in her face. "Here try this."

"Ewww. No."

"Come one. Don't be a chicken."

"I'm not eating that!" She tried to push this off.

He wormed away from her and rubbed the dough off on her nose. Her face turned bright red. She snatched a spoon off the counter and hit him with it. There was no way she could hurt a him, being a vampire, but he fake flinched and pulled away. His acting turned her momentary frustration into another fit of laugher.

They rolled out cookies hand shaped into little men and threw them in the oven. He checked his phone again before kneading the muscles in her neck a second time. She rubbed his hand. After another few minutes the timer went off and they pulled out the cookies.

"Well that looks…"

"Like dead bodies," he finished. The cookie men had melted out and looked more like rows of zombies.

She poked him in the ribs. "You try it."

He shook his head. "Can't. Vampire remember. I don't do solid food."

"Convenient excuse," she scoffed.

"Yes. Because I became a vampire just to get out of eating." She flinched. Maybe that was too harsh of a comment. He wrapped his arms around her so she knew he wasn't trying to be mean. He was still a bit of a monster. A bit scary at times. He never wanted her upset or worried about anything she said or thought. "Up to you, my dear. Try one."

"Hmmm." She smashed her lips together several times before finally trying a cookie. Her lips pulled back as she chewed. "Well it's not bad."

He laughed. "Well I can't say I make a good cook."

She stopped still for a moment. Her breathing even ceased for one second.

"What's wrong? What is it?"

She leaned her head back against his chest, waves of red hair spilled over his arms. "Thank you. Thank you for trying so hard."

"That's my job. You know that."

"Still my guardian vampire."

"Always."

Her eyes drifted back to the windows. Wads of paper littered the floor and their tiny tissue decorations half his in the shadows above the window. She still had a bit of sadness to her. Something that seems to be eating at her.

"What is it?" He turned her around to face him so he could see her eyes.

She didn't meet his gaze again.

"Now. Now. Don't start hiding things from me. What's wrong."

"I guess I still want a tree. Maybe we can get one next-"

A knock came from the door, cutting her off. She jumped, backing up to the counter. He caught her arms and ran his hand up to her shoulder. "It's ok." He glanced once more at his phone before heading to the door.

She followed him half way, giving him a confused look. He grinned and pulled the door open.

"It took long enough," Fish whined. His friend Fish, a wiry guy with large glasses, pulled a large box into the apartment. "Hey, Ada."

"Fish- I mean Chip. what are you doing here?"

"Bringing the tree. What…" He glanced at Nikolai and grinned. "Ohh, you didn't tell her."

"Tell me what?"

"Nikolai texted me earlier, begging me to bring a tree here."

A larger man followed Fish into the apartment. He had a grey shirt with several mustard stains on them and held two shopping bags. "And he got ahold of me to bring us some food. I had some leftover cake from the shop too I brought."

"Alfredo, you too." She put her hands together. Her eyes twinkled as she looked over to Nikolai. The strong savory smell of sandwiches and cake mixed into the air.

The three men drug the tree in and pulled it from the box. Nikolai and Fish worked on the branches.

Alfredo grinned as he pulled foot out and laid it on the coffee table. "Nikolai, don't you own a table?"

He laughed. "Ummm. I don't know. Maybe it broke."

Ada grinned back at him. They two men didn't know his secret side and he knew she would never give him away. She was the one person in the world he trusted with his secret.

Another knock came from the door. He tensed with excitement, hoping it was the last thing. The one thing that would make this perfect.

"What now?" asked Ada.

"Just wait." He shook as he reached for the door. Anticipation and worry coursed through him. Could it be that perfect? Would this really work? He pulled the door open.

Marcus scowled back at him. He still wore a suit with an 1800s flair. "Here." He grunted and shoved a small back at Nikolai.

"Marcus," Ada screeched.

He lifted his head to her and for a moment his eyes glowed. Ada sucked a quick breath and glanced at the other two men.

Nikolai waved Marcus out of the door. "Thanks. We'll talk later." He slammed the door on him.

From Ada's expression, he could tell she was just as worried as he was about exposing his secret. It wasn't like him to bring in another vampire or risk humans seeing him. But today was different. Today was special. He would do anything to make their first Christmas memorable.

"What's going on?" A light came from the windows, distracting her. She turned to a fully lit up Christmas tree. Her eyes went wide and filled with tears. "It's a tree."

He chuckled. "Yes, it is."

Fish and Alfredo looked at each other and inched towards the door. "Ummm, don't know exactly what is going on, but we have to go."

Alfredo nodded in agreement. "Glad to help you to. Merry Christmas."

The pair let themselves out.

"I don't understand," said Ada. "Why did Marcus come? That's a huge risk."

He took her hand in his. "Yes. But worth it." He turned her palm up and put the small rectangular box in her hands. "But I could not let you have a Christmas without a present."

Her hands shook. Happy tears released from her twinkling eyes. She opened the tiny box. Christmas lights glinted off a band of diamonds and rubies. "Is this real."

"Of course. I would never get you something fake." He took it from her and clasped the bracelet around her wrist. "It's not as beautiful as you, but I thought you would like it."

"Wait? Did you already have this?"

He nodded. "Marcus has been holding onto a few things for me. This one, is special. It was meant for someone else once, that I cared about. I…" He paused to steady his voice. "I never thought I would find another I would care more for. But I have you." He looked up, making sure to have her full attention. "I wouldn't want anyone else to have it."

Her choked happy gasp made him grin. She threw her arms around him. Warm. Alive. Loving. Everything his undead heart had always desired. No more. She turned her head against his chest to see the tree and let a contented sigh.

Their first Christmas would be one she would never forget.

Larry Brown

Larry Brown is a writer who looks for the depth of a story and tells it as honestly as possible. He has written over 200 short stories and is working on a novel. He has traveled the world while in the military and brings his vast experience to his stories. Local publications have included historical and op-ed pieces.

Learn more about Larry at:

www.facebook.com/ruralhistorybuffsmarioncounty

Anna's Bells

Cold wind blew snow in the parking lot below the hospital window. Tree limbs swayed in the icy morning, as blackbirds huddled in flocks to ward off the winter chill. Few cars were parked, the empty spaces receiving the full impact of last night's storm. The morning sun began its rise to spread rays on the scene, casting long shadows against the white landscape.

In the warmth of the waiting room, Sara stood at the picture window with her grandmother's shawl wrapped around her shoulders and watched, without seeing, the day unfold below her. She held back tears. She wanted to be a strong woman, especially today. It was Christmas and Anna needed her.

"Mrs. Collins?" A distant voice asked. "Mrs. Collins, we need you to sign some papers." A nurse came into the room, sat at a table then laid down her documents. "We could sit here. It's just a few things we need to cover."

Sara turned from the window and sat down next to the woman. Pulling the papers closer, she automatically signed without reading them. The other woman, her clean uniform contrasting with Sara's rumpled clothes, smiled at her and patted her shoulder.

"I peeked in on your daughter while looking for you. For a six year old, she seems to be handling things well."

Sara attempted a return smile but the effort felt a waste of time to her. "Yes, she's doing better. A new drug was added to her others. Always hope you know."

"Hope is what we all have. Family is a strong medicine too. Are you here by yourself?"

"My uncle was supposed to come. But the storm will delay him, if he can get through at all. My parents are gone. Uncle Buck is all that's left." She didn't elaborate on the impact her uncle had on her life. He was the only family left now. After her parents died, he took her in and helped her to get through school, then through the loss of her husband. Without him she shuddered to think how she would have survived. Sara stood, putting those thought away for now.

"I've going back to Anna. She was asleep and thought I would take a break, but she should be up by now."

"My name is Kitty, Mrs. Collins. If I can help let me know." Kitty picked up the documents and walked with Sara down the hall to Anna's room. At the doorway Sara leaned against the frame and watched Anna stroke the fur of her favorite toy, a stuffed dog. The IV's infusion lines linked bags of liquid to the little girl's arms, making any movement uncomfortable. Seeing her mom brought a wave of her hand.

"Mommy. There you are. Sugar missed you. Where were you?"

Sara managed a smile. "Oh, just stretching my legs. How are you feeling?"

Anna held up Sugar, her toy dog and wiggled him in the air. "We're doing real good Mommy." Sara knew better. But she was the mother of a strong daughter and she was grateful for that. Being a single mom meant being everything to Anna, but in turn, Anna was everything to her.

"Anna, you know what today is?"

"Nope, do you?"

Sara laughed. Not out loud, but in relief that Anna could still be herself, the precious child that she loved so much.

"Yes I do." Sara walked to Anna's side and petted Sugar. "It's Christmas and I think Santa Clause is coming by later today. What do you think about that?"

"Will he have anything for Sugar?"

"Bet he will and something for you too of course." Anna smiled. Sara knew she had to tell her about the new medicine. The tough part of being her parent was telling her the truth. Sara smoothed down Anna's unruly curls and sat.

"You are getting new medicine today Anna. I don't know how it will make you feel, but we have hope."

"Is that my present from Santa Clause?"

Sara let herself laugh out loud. "No silly. Santa brings fun things. The doctors are sharing their new medicine. Just for you."

Anna's eyes closed, her lips a smile. It didn't take much to fatigue the little girl.

Sara sat back and dozed herself. An image of a long gone Christmas, her as a little girl and her family sitting around an organ. Her dad played it and Uncle Buck had his brass bells. The Christmas bells brought joy every holiday season to her family. The warmth of a fireplace and the pine smell of the tree and the music among a loving family, a place that Sara missed.

The day went as normal as it could. Nurses coming in and out, changing bags every few hours, people walking up and down the hallway some with their kids holding onto to IV poles, their parents hovering close. It was becoming routine to Anna and Sara, a never ending drama of life and death.

The sun had made its way to Anna's side of the building, warmer rays highlighting her room. Sara woke to see Anna resting peacefully in her white bed and decided to take a walk. She returned to the waiting room, sat and hung her head. The never ending toll of caring for Anna weighing her down.

The view from the window was now of black asphalt with white strips and naked trees with roosting black birds huddling again for warmth. Behind her, Sara felt the hospital beginning to return to its somber night time level. In the distance she heard the chimes of bells ringing a Christmas tune.

Sara smiled to herself when she realized the jingle was one that Uncle Buck often rang at Christmas. The soft melody, the gentle way he shook each one to bring out its refrain, his eyes that laughed in the joy of happy children. That life was gone as was her parents. She frowned and turned from the window. Now was not a time to be mournful, Anna needed her.

The Christmas carol solo grew louder as she walked down the corridor. In the hallway, a few children clutching their IV poles were also walking towards Anna's room. She weaved around them and stopped at the door way, her breathing halting and her heart racing.

She gasped and held her hands to her face. She couldn't speak and tears flowed down her cheeks. Anna sat upright in her bed, her eyes glowing with a life that Sara had not seen for a long time. Beside her a man stood over a serving tray covered with glistening brass bells, ringing each one in a perfect refrain of "Christmas Bells".

"Oh, Uncle Buck, you made it." Sara leaped towards her uncle and hugged him. "Thank you, thank you." Her eyes were clouded by tears, but the enthralled look on Anna's face was all the thanks that Uncle Buck needed.

"Had to come Sara, no snow no wind was going to stop me. It's Christmas and you both needed me. Its family that makes this holiday special you know."

Michael Van Natta

Michael is a long-time resident of Knoxville and Dr. at the local hospital. Mike has run the Marion County Writers Workshop for many years, helping many new and published authors. In his spare time, he runs his winery and tasting room, Nearwood Winery. His novel, Leo's Birds came out in 2012 and he is currently working on several new novels.

Learn more about Mike at:

Amazon – Leo's Birds

thewriteplace.biz/product/leos-birds/

A Christmas Accident

There were lots of things in his kitchen. Over the years, especially in better times, he'd bought this meat grinder or that skillet at some flea market, purchased this flour sifter and this coffee pot at that garage sale on Fifth Street, acquired that double boiler from his brother's estate. In better times, he'd built a kitchen his wife had loved. Merryweather Parks too, loved his kitchen and through the years cooked there for the two of them; stews and soups, bread and torts, egg soufflés and collard greens. In recent memory, though, it had been mostly just cold porridge, a fried egg on toast, maybe a heated up tin of soup. Sometimes, more often now, he'd drag himself to his small bedroom, lay his aching body on the thin mattress, wait for his weight to come to a resting place and fall asleep having eaten nothing.

His cold-water flat was lit only by a holiday candle flickering on a saucer set on the small kitchen table. He'd placed a photograph of his wife on the table too and next to it, the now empty glass of a cheap wine he'd splurged on as a gift to himself. Danny, his dog lay by the stove.

The snow had piled up on the windowsill, gathering at the corners and climbing up the side glazing. Frosty glass blurred his view of the street four stories below. The cobbler's entrance had been shoveled out but Habber's

General Store on the other side was drifted completely shut. One person trudged through the driving snow, hooded and hunched over against the wind, man or woman, he couldn't tell, making way up the gentle slope toward the row houses. No vehicles moved. There would be no crashes tonight. Those parked along the street wore hoods as well, of heavy winter white. In the faint light of gray fading evening, Merryweather made to guess their make and model: here a Ford, there a Chevy, there a Studebaker.

Many men had jumped from such heights, he knew, or higher. James Little from accounting had jumped. A.G. Pierce, the vice president, had jumped.

"Hell of a day for a blizzard," he said to night. He shivered, stood and clanged open the hot round iron door of the pot-bellied stove, tossed in a chuck of gnarled wood he'd brought from the woods. He found it odd that he talked to his possessions but it went some distance to relieve the emptiness he felt. "A year ago," he said, closing the stove with an oven mitt. "To this very day."

Merryweather, at forty two, had lost the love of his life on Christmas Day the year before. It had been a long battle and mostly, he was glad Julia no longer had to suffer. When it had become obvious that the cancer was too far gone, Merryweather began collecting the best memories of her, a smile here and there, the way she still made their bed, the flowers on the long dining table arranged just so. Alone in the house, during her occasional stays in the hospital, he methodically began looking back, cataloging their togetherness, bundling the memories of vacations and horseback riding, of movies and late night dinners, of house cleaning and afternoon walks, painting the walls of the nursery that would never be occupied, bringing home the new puppy, shopping in Chicago, art festivals in Kansas City, boating in the Ozarks, her as bridesmaid at her sister's wedding, collections of jumbled memories of an almost perfect life, yet to be sorted through.

In those better times - those heady times, the newspapers called them - there had been money and loads of it. They had lived in the country home then, west of the city. She had not known these dark times. The memory of her, laying peaceful amid silk and velvet, her last resting place, adorned in her best blue dress with her pearl necklace, red lipstick on her almost smiling lips, was one he knew he would keep, had to keep.

On the top of the stove, he'd set a pot of oyster stew to warm. The small room had taken on the scent of the sea. His wife's family in Omaha had always had made oyster stew for Christmas. A tradition, she'd told him.

Merryweather's own family had no such traditions and lived in far-away South Carolina. Julia and he spent nearly every holiday in Omaha.

He'd bought the oysters and the milk and the potatoes at Haber's yesterday after he'd walked home from his job at the newspaper and before the snow started to fall. He missed his automobile, a Chrysler Stanza he kept shined and full of petrol, in the same way he missed most things. At least, he told himself, he had the job. It wasn't much - Copy Boy, it was called - but it put food on the table.

He went back to the window seat with a fresh glass of wine, gazed down at the soft expanse of white darkness. The street lights had come on, spotlighting circles of snow, drifting and shifting, spitting snow dust from sharp edges in the fierce gloom. The man with the hood had turned around, perhaps though better of it, and was stepping slow through the knee-high snow, back to wherever, the six or seven wrong-way footsteps already nearly filled in. No storefront was lit, nothing else moved.

He thought of Julia, the Christmas holidays they'd celebrated together, twelve if he had to include the year before. He'd wished her Merry Christmas that morning but she never was able to leave the bed, her strength depleted. She'd meant to wear the blue dress with her pearls but she was never got to.

Below, the man tripped and fell headfirst. Merryweather rose, watched as he struggled in the more than foot of what was apparently very wet and heavy snow. At first, Merryweather thought the man would just push himself up, as he would have done. Soon, however, it became apparent that no amount of struggling was going to be successful. Merryweather went to his closet.

The night air was cold but not overly so. Still the wind-driven snow bit into his cheeks. Though the man was right below his window, it took a few minutes to get to him from the building's entrance. The snow was indeed heavy and wet.

The man was laying on his side, curled into a ball, and was whimpering, crying almost.

"Hey, are you alright?" he said when he got close. "Here, let me help you."

Merryweather expected to see an old and fragile man but instead, the woman lifted her head and he saw her wet face under a hood of fur.

"Oh, thank you, thank you," the woman said. "I can't seem to get up and now I'm so tired. I thought I'd die out here." She was shivering uncontrollably.

It was an easy thing for the two of them to get her back up on her feet. She pointed across and up the street "I just live right over there."

Arm and arm they went, toward her house. "I was just delivering this," she held out a small box wrapped in red paper with a red bow. "To my niece for Christmas. She lives only a block down the street but I couldn't make it. The snow was too deep."

When they reached her door, she asked him in to warm up before going home. I make a great Hot Toddy," she said, stepping in.

"No," Merryweather said. "I'd love to Miss, but I have Oyster stew cooking at home."

"Oh. Ok. But at least tell me your name? I'm Jenny Burns," she held out a red hand.

"I'm Merryweather Parks. I just live right across the street. How about you write down the address of your niece and I'll deliver your package to her before I go home?"

"Oh, no. You've done enough already. You, you practically saved my life, after all."

"It's no trouble, Ms. Burns, really. Might as well make your niece a little happier this Christmas."

"Please call me Jenny." She handed him the red box and hastily scribbled the address on an old envelope, smiled and handed it to him.

"You are too kind, Mr. Parks," she said when he pulled up his collar. "I insist that you take a rain check on my Hot Toddy. I do make a very good one."

"I will. And you must call me Merry." He immediately saw the irony of his words.

"I will! Merry Christmas, Merry!" She laughed like a little girl and Merryweather thought it very endearing that she covered her mirth with a hand over her mouth. "Merry Christmas to you, as well."

A half an hour later, Merryweather Parks was back in his flat, sitting at his table, finishing his glass of wine and feeling warm inside for good deeds done. He was halfway through his bowl of oyster stew. The oysters were somewhat tough but they were tasty and passable. Then chewing, he felt something rock hard between his teeth. He reached in with his fingers and retrieved the offender and there, between his fingers, a shining pearl the size of a pea.

He raised his head and laughed, maybe for the first time in a year. He laughed and laughed and when he settled down, he set the pearl on the table next to the picture of his wife.

"Merry Christmas, Julia," he whispered.

Printed in Great Britain
by Amazon